Supernana

By Eva Byrne

Abrams Books for Young Readers

New York

Sharper than a pair of knitting needles . . .

Stronger than sticky tape . . .

It's SUPERNANA!

Late for school again?
Supernana can turn back time.

She can do anything! Like help out at the science fair
and bake chocolate chip cookies for everybody to share.

Supernana is
out of this world!

Whether there's a spaceship
in distress . . .

. . . or an octopus in a terrible mess . . .

Supernana's on it.

When you need to make a quick escape,
Supernana's got your back.

Whatever the problem, Supernana knows
ice cream is always a good solution!

No matter what you need, she's got you covered.
Everybody loves Supernana!

Everybody except . . . Madame Le Flea!

This tiny terror has been working on her latest invention.

Madame Le Flea and her Shrinkalizer descend on the city.

Nothing tall is safe!

Watch out!

A tiny dancer.

A pocket-sized giraffe.

"SUPERNANA, WHERE ARE YOU?"

Have no fear!

Supernana is here!

Madame Le Flea's got
nothing on this superhero.

It takes all of Supernana's mighty powers, but she saves the city from Madame Le Flea.

"Nana, I think bedtime stories are your superpower."

For my parents, Evelyn and Larry, my very own superheroes. xoxo

The illustrations in this book were created with pencil and Photoshop.

Cataloging-in-Publication Data has been applied for
and may be obtained from the Library of Congress.

ISBN 978-1-4197-5016-8

Text and illustrations © 2021 Eva Byrne
Book design by Jade Rector

Printed and bound in China
10 9 8 7 6 5 4 3 2 1

Abrams Books for Young Readers are available at special discounts when purchased in quantity for premiums
and promotions as well as fundraising or educational use. Special editions can also be created to specification.
For details, contact specialsales@abramsbooks.com or the address below.

ABRAMS The Art of Books
195 Broadway, New York, NY 10007
abramsbooks.com